Niles and Bradford

Basketball Shots

By: Marcy Blesy

Cover design by Cormar Covers

Follow my blog for information about upcoming books or short stories.

Chapter 1:

Niles is not the newest kid anymore. He started school with his baseball friends. The best thing about this school is that there are always so many things to do. And if the school does not offer something Niles wants to do, the local community center probably does. *You will never be bored. There will always be things to do. There will always be fun to have,* says his mom. She is very confident. But Niles is not so sure about his newest sport—basketball. There are only two things that Niles feels like he can count on when it comes to trying a new sport. One thing he knows is that he is not afraid to try something new. He works hard. Sometimes the hard work pays off, and he does well. He scores a goal. He makes a basket. He gets a hole in one. Sometimes he works hard and doesn't do well, but he likes playing either way.

The other thing Niles can count on is his best friend Bradford. Bradford is Niles's pet dragon. Bradford is not an imaginary friend. He's very much a real, orange, foot tall dragon. He is so good at staying hidden that no one has seen him except for Niles. That includes Niles's mom and dad and big sister Nora. There have been close calls—like the one time that Mom came into the bedroom to put Niles's socks away. Bradford was sleeping in a pair of fuzzy, red socks in a drawer. Red is his favorite color. He also likes to sleep. Mom screamed when she picked up the sock to move aside to make room for the new socks. *Niles, what are you hiding in your sock drawer? Get in here.* Niles ran into the room as fast as he could. He knew exactly what Mom was yelling about. So did Bradford. He went *poof* as soon as he heard Mom scream and disappeared. He was hiding under the bed now. *What's going on, Mom?* Niles tried to be cool. *Pick that sock up and show me what is inside.* Niles grabbed the socks. He picked them up. Thank goodness they were light. Bradford was not inside. Niles shook out the socks to show that nothing was there. Mom scratched her head and talked to herself. *I must be losing my mind.* There would be other close calls with Bradford. But so far, he's Niles's special secret.

No, trying a new sport is not always easy. But choosing the easy way is boring. Plus, a lot of his friends will be at basketball tryouts. He won't be alone. Niles is ready.

Chapter 2:

Tryouts for the Clearview Turtles are today. Niles learned that the *Turtles* mascot was picked over fifty years ago. A turtle laid its eggs in a pile of rocks outside the front door of the new school. When the turtles were born, they lived in a small pond next to the school. During the year that they lived there, all the sports' teams did well. The basketball, football, and baseball teams all won the state title. The school board voted to change the school mascot to the *Turtles* even though another state title has never been won since.

There are nineteen boys who show up to basketball tryouts. Tad, Luke, Nick, Vinnie, Sammy, Scotty, Otis, and Rashid from the baseball team are there along with ten other boys including Niles. The coach is a young man. He looks like he just got out of school himself. He looks like he could have been on the high school team last year. Niles wonders if he has ever coached before. Unlike Coach Fartzer from the baseball team, this Coach does not have a name that makes the kids laugh.

The whistle blows. "Come over to the bench, boys. Have a seat. My name is Coach Anderson. Thanks for being here. Let me tell you how this is going to work. To give playing time to the most kids possible during our basketball season, I can only take ten kids on the team. I am very sorry. Michael Jordan was one of the best basketball players of all time. He did not make his high school varsity team as soon as he wanted to. He never gave up. I do not want you to give up if you do not make the team."

No one moves. But lots of eyes dart around the bench. People are thinking about who might be cut from the team. Niles plays basketball in his driveway at home with his dad. He has never been on a team before. Some of these boys played on the eight-year-old team last year.

"We will warm up first. Get on the line under the basket. When I blow the whistle, I want you to run to the other side of the gym. Wait for the whistle, and I will blow again. Then run back," says Coach Anderson.

Everyone lines up. "This is awful," says Tad. Coach cannot hear him.

"You don't like to run, Tad?" asks Scotty. Scotty asks lots of questions.

"No, Scotty, I do not like to run. I like to shoot. I like to dribble. I do not like to run," says Tad.

"Well, you had better get used to running," says Luke. "You cannot play basketball without a lot of running."

Before Tad can respond, Coach Anderson blows the whistle. Everyone runs.

"This is...awesome!" says Rashid. Just like in baseball season, Rashid is always smiling.

Tad rolls his eyes.

The whistle blows again. "Grab a basketball. Take some shots to warm up. We will practice lay-ups and free throws today."

"Do you shoot a free throw from the line in the middle of the court?" Scotty asks Coach Anderson.

Coach gives Scotty a funny look. "Are you making a joke?" he asks.

"No. Does it sound like a joke—I mean, is it some joke I don't know?"

Niles pulls Scotty to the floor. "Grab a basketball, Scotty. I will show you the free throw line."

The boys practice shooting. Luke sinks the most shots. They go into the basket smooth as glass. He likes to shoot far away from the basket. Nick shoots well, too. Some of the boys look like they have never touched a basketball before. The rest of the boys are somewhere in the middle.

Coach Anderson throws a ball at Luke. He catches it. "Show everyone what a lay-up looks like."

The balls stop bouncing while the boys watch Luke. He starts running from the side of the court. He dribbles the basketball as he runs. When he gets close to the basket, he raises the ball as he shoots it. He aims for the backboard. The ball falls into the net. He makes it look easy.

The boys line up to take their turns, over and over. Niles misses his first two lay-ups but makes his last three. Scotty shoots well. The Coach is taking notes on a piece of paper on his clipboard.

Nick shows the boys how to shoot free throws. The basket is a long way from the free throw line for some of the kids. They are not seven feet tall like pro basketball players.

"Okay, boys. Now I am going to divide you into teams. I know you have not learned any plays or much else, really, but I want to see how you might play as a team. Dribble the ball, pass the ball, shoot the ball. Got it? Any questions?"

Scotty's hand flies up.

"Yes, Scotty?"

"Do I get to shoot a free throw?" Scotty is surprisingly good at shooting free throws.

"Only if you get fouled by another player."

"Okay. What's a fou…"

"We will go over that as needed. Today I am looking at your skills, your ability to learn from what I tell you, how well you play with others."

Coach Anderson does not ask for more questions. "Let's go!"

Niles, Luke, Vinnie, Rashid, and a boy named Abe are on a team. Abe is also new this year. He has played basketball before. He makes a lot of baskets.

"Thirty seconds to go," says Coach Anderson.

Vinnie throws the ball in from the sideline. Abe catches the ball, dribbles, and passes the ball to Niles. Niles dribbles the ball and passes the ball to Luke. Luke dribbles past Otis, who is on the other team. He tries a lay-up but misses. Rashid gets a rebound. He passes the ball to Niles.

"5-4-3-2…"

Niles shoots the ball at the buzzer. It rolls about the rim of the basket and falls out— bouncing loudly on the floor below. The score is tied. There are no overtimes in tryouts.

"I will post the ten boys who made the team on the gym door tomorrow before school. Remember that no one is a loser. Try again or try something else. There is something for all of you out there. Keep your heads up. Have a nice night."

When Niles gets home, Bradford is waiting on his bed.

"You are supposed to be in my dresser drawer!" Niles says to Bradford.

"You're grumpy," says Bradford. He does a backwards somersault. "Ta-daaaa!" Bradford sticks out his little arms. This is the time that Niles usually claps wildly. Not tonight.

"I don't think I made the team." Niles hangs his basketball bag in the closet. Maybe he can use it for the next team he tries out for.

"How come?" asks Bradford. He jumps off the bed and hops onto Niles's foot. Niles is wearing red socks.

Niles kicks him off. "I missed the last shot of the game."

Bradford uses his teeth to pull a tissue out of the box from the nightstand. He takes it to Niles.

"What is that for?" he asks.

"You are sad. You need a tissue," says Bradford. "That's what your mom gives Nora when she's sad."

Niles smiles—a little smile. "Thanks, Bradford. You are a good friend."

"I know. Now, please get me a peanut butter sandwich. I am starving! And *no jelly!*"

Chapter 3:

Niles *closes* his eyes. He takes a deep breath. The list of the boys who made the Clearview Turtles basketball team is hanging on the gym door. A group of boys are pushing and shoving around him. He hears many things.

Yes!

Awesome!

That stinks.

Whatever.

And also silence.

Niles wonders how he will react. Finally, he stands in front of the list. He opens his eyes. There, on the bottom of the list he sees it. *Niles Woodson.* He rubs his eyes. He cannot believe it. He smiles. So does Bradford. He peeks out of Niles's backpack. He does not come to school often. He knows better. But Niles might have needed him today.

The first practice is after school. Lots of high fives and back slapping happens.

"Niles, good to see you here," says Tad. "I knew you would make the team."

"Thanks, Tad. I wasn't so sure."

"Can you believe it? Can you *just* believe it?" asks Scotty.

"To be honest, Scotty, I really can't," says Tad.

Niles shakes his head at Tad as if to say *you should not have said that.*

Tad grabs a basketball and runs off to the court.

Niles, Rashid, Luke, Nick, Sammy, Vinnie, Scotty, Tad, Abe, and Cole made the team. Niles tries not to think about his friends who did not.

Coach Anderson runs the boys for the first ten minutes of practice—a lot. While the boys are running, Bradford watches cheerleading practice. They are having their tryouts today at the far end of the gym. This is the first year there is a cheerleading team for the nine-year-old basketball team. The school wants to prepare the kids early for competing in cheer competitions in middle school. Kyle from the baseball team is trying out, too. Bradford thinks that's cool. He hopes Kyle makes the team. But Bradford *really* hopes the red-headed girl with the long wavy hair makes the team. *Anything* with red makes Bradford happy.

"Boys! Let's shoot some lay-ups. Luke show them how it's done again," says Coach Anderson.

Luke dribbles the ball to the basket and aims at the backboard. The ball goes in. He does this a few more times. The ball goes in every time.

When Niles shoots the ball during the lay-up drill, he misses more baskets than he makes. He is frustrated. The same thing happens during other shooting drills. Nick shows the boys how to shoot from the three-point line. The same thing happens during this shooting drill. Niles misses more than he makes. Even Scotty makes Niles look bad during the free throw drill. Maybe that's why Scotty made the team. He can sure sink those shots from the line.

Bradford wiggles in Niles's backpack. *Go. GO-GO! Shoot. SHOOT-SHOOT! Win. WIN! WIN!* Then he turns around and shakes his tail.

"No, No, No," shouts Coach Anderson.

That doesn't sound like a good cheer thinks Bradford. He wiggles Niles's backpack closer to the court.

"You have to use the backboard, boys. It gives you something to aim for. Hit the square on the backboard, and you make the basket—at least that is what is supposed to happen," says Coach Anderson.

The boys dribble the ball, pass the ball, and shoot the ball. They do this drill over and over. Bradford is bored. He has a plan. He unzips the backpack. He crawls out. He turns the backpack around and pushes it up. He stands behind it where he cannot be seen.

"*Hey, Hey, Go, Go, Don't you stop. Don't be slow. You—can—do—it! Hey!*

He repeats the cheer, louder this time.

"*Hey, Hey, Go, Go, Don't you stop. Don't be slow. You—can—do—it! Hey!*"

Coach Anderson blows his whistle. "What is that noise?"

Nile stops running. He listens.

"*Hey, Hey, Go, Go, Don't you stop. Don't be slow. You—can—do—it! Hey!*"

Oh no, thinks Niles. *Bradford.*

"*Hey, Hey, Go, Go, Don't you stop. Don't be slow. You—can—do—it! Hey!*"

"*Hey, Hey, Go, Go, Don't you stop. Don't be slow. You—can—do—it! Hey!*"

The noise is clearly coming from Niles's red backpack. He thinks about what to do. "It's—uh—it's my cellphone, Coach," says Niles. "Sorry."

"You have a cellphone?" asks Scotty.

"You have a cheer as your ringtone?" asks Tad.

"Shut off that phone," says Coach Anderson.

Niles runs to his backpack.

Poof! Bradford jumps back inside, but Niles knows.

He unzips his bag, reaches inside, and turns Bradford over so that he is facing Niles. "You are in so much trouble," Niles whispers. "Do not move."

Niles has never been so embarrassed. And mad—very, very mad.

Chapter 4:

Niles gives Bradford the silent treatment at home. He is still mad.

"Please, can I have a peanut butter sandwich?" begs Bradford. "I will be good. I was just trying to help."

Niles turns over in his bed. He flips the page of the magazine he is not really reading.

Bradford *poofs* on top of the magazine. Niles flicks him off with his finger.

"Ouch!" says Bradford.

Niles gets off the bed and flops into the beanbag chair on his floor. He tosses his basketball in the air, over and over.

Bradford *poofs* to the beanbag. "You can't give me the silent treatment forever. I am your best friend."

Niles does not stop throwing the ball. So, Bradford kicks it away with his little foot. The ball crashes into his Star Wars lego set, sending the pieces crashing to the floor. "Uh, oh. Sorry, Niles." He *poofs* under the covers. He peeks out to watch Niles's reaction.

Niles stands up, changes into his practice jersey, grabs his basketball shoes and bag, and slams the door. He shoots hoops from the driveway over and over—alone.

Bradford has never been so sad since he was abandoned in the woods by his former owner years ago when he grew too old for a pet dragon. Before

Niles saved him.

Chapter 5:

By the end of the first week of practice, things are getting better for the team. Luke, Nick, Tad, Cole, and Abe are the stand-out players. They will be the starting five. Niles, Rashid, Scotty, Sammy and Vinnie are the second-string team. Coach tells them they have an important job. They support the starters. They give them good competition in practice. And some of them will be subs for the starters during the games. They always need to be ready. Niles does not give up. He works hard every single practice. He even makes a free throw during a practice game. Things are looking up.

"Nice effort today," says Coach Anderson. "You are improving every day, Niles."

"Thanks, Coach."

Abe invites everyone to his house for a bonfire. Niles is happy for a break. He has been doing nothing but going to school and practicing basketball. Since he still won't talk to Bradford, he has been kind of lonely.

Bradford is lonely, too. He only wants to help his best friend, all the time. So, when Niles leaves for the bonfire, Bradford makes a new plan. On a cartoon once, Bradford watched a boy who was having trouble roller skating. The boy put jet packs onto the back of his skates. Fire blazed out from the skates. The boy took off and never looked back. He was having a lot of fun. *And* he looked like a great roller skater. Bradford did not have jet packs. But he did have fire. Time to improve those basketball shoes.

"Rashid, what do you think about Coach?" asks Scotty. They are sitting around a bonfire in Abe's backyard.

Rashid smiles, as usual. "He's cool. He seems serious. I think he likes to win."

"There's nothing wrong with liking to win," says Tad.

"It's not everything, though," says Rashid.

"Easy for you to say. You're not in the starting five," says Tad

"Don't be such a jerk, Tad," says Luke.

Tad gets up from the picnic table in Abe's backyard. At least he doesn't try to continue the fight.

The boys play hide-and-seek in the dark. They use flashlights. Team bonding at its best.

Niles gets home happy. He is happy that he has made new friends in Clearview. He is happy to be part of a team. Before he climbs into bed, he decides to check on Bradford. Maybe it is time to stop the silent treatment and forgive him. *He was just trying to help*, thinks Niles.

Niles opens the dresser drawer. Bradford is not inside the red fuzzy socks, his favorite bed. *That's weird*, thinks Niles.

A funny smell catches the attention of Niles. He picks up some of his clothes from the floor. At the bottom of a pile he sees his bright red basketball shoes—his brand-new basketball shoes. Smoke seeps through the holes in the heels of both shoes. Niles grabs his shoes and stomps them on the floor to stop the flow of smoke. His eyes dart around the room.

"Bradford!"

Chapter 6:

The first game of the season is today. The crowd is mostly full of the players' families. And the cheerleaders' families. Coach Anderson looks nervous. He keeps blowing his whistle at the boys. They run through mini-drills before the game. They work on passing, dribbling, and shooting. The team is nervous, too. The Bayside Bears look tough. They are tall. They are fast.

The referees call the starting players on both teams to the middle of the court.

"Be good sports, boys," says the head referee. "What we say goes. Do not argue. That goes for the coaches, too." He looks at Coach Anderson and the coach of the Bayside Bears.

Everyone nods in agreement.

Luke, Tad, Nick, Abe, and Cole run to their spots on the floor. The referee blows his whistle. Cole, the tallest player on our team, and a tall player from the Bayside Bears team jump for the ball. Cole tips the basketball to Tad. Tad still does not like to run. He dribbles the ball down the court while walking. Even Coach Anderson's yelling doesn't make him move faster.

Nick makes the first basket. The ball moves up and down the court. Niles and his teammates Sammy, Vinnie, Rashid, and Scotty sit on the bench. They cheer for their friends. Niles cheers especially loud. He wears an old pair of basketball shoes that Rashid's older brother used to wear.

They are a little small. He does not complain, though. He can't. His mom is still mad. She thinks that Niles burned his own shoes because he was playing with matches. Nothing could be more wrong. Niles knows better than to play with matches. But he had to agree with her thoughts. How could he tell her that his pet dragon Bradford used fire to burn a hole in his shoes thinking that he could create flames that would make him run faster. The idea is so silly. But that's what Bradford told Niles. Then Niles picked Bradford up by the tail and put him in the basement. And every time Bradford *poofed* himself back to Niles's bedroom, Niles picked him up by the tail again and put him back in the basement. This happened seven times before Bradford gave up. He curled inside an old red sleeping bag and cried.

At halftime, the Bayside Bears are winning 18-10. Coach Anderson seems pleased even though they are losing. "Don't be afraid to shoot the ball, boys. You can do this."

"Scotty, go in for Nick," says Coach Anderson.

"Me, Coach? You want *me* to go in?"

"You heard me. *Go!*"

Scotty runs to the check-in table to tell them he is going in for Nick. When the whistle blows next, Scotty and Nick switch places. Nick gets a drink of water. Scotty gets called for traveling with the ball. He forgot to dribble the ball. But then he gets fouled, and he gets to shoot a free throw. He makes the basket. The crowd goes crazy. Rashid is smiling so big, it's almost like he made the basket himself.

Vinnie goes in for Tad in the fourth quarter. He shoots a couple of times but misses. Tad goes back into the game. Sammy goes in for Abe. He makes a nice lay-up. Rashid and Niles stay on the bench, but they cheer for their team. There will be other games. Poor Rashid sat on the bench during most of the baseball season, too.

The buzzer marks the end of the game. The Bayside Bears beat the Clearview Turtles 38-22. The boys slap hands with the other team. Good sportsmanship ends the game.

"Nice first game, boys," says Coach Anderson. "Be ready to work hard at practice tomorrow."

Niles and his family get ice cream after the game. But Niles doesn't feel like eating. Something is missing. In the past, whenever things have not gone well for Niles, his best friend has cheered him up. Now his best friend is locked in the basement. Maybe it is time for a talk.

Chapter 7:

Bradford is sound asleep in a bowling ball bag. The red ball is rolling freely on the basement floor.

"Bradford." Niles whispers his best friend's name. "Bradford."

Bradford lifts his head. His eyes have never looked so sad. Then he rubs his eyes. He sits up when he sees Niles.

"Hey, buddy," says Niles. "I think we need to talk."

"Does this talk end with me getting a peanut butter sandwich? Because I am fed up with eating the spiders and bugs I find in this basement. No flavor. They have no flavor at all."

Niles laughs. "Yes, it can end in peanut butter sandwiches."

Bradford hops next to Niles on the couch. "How did your first game go?"

"We lost."

"That's okay," says Bradford. "Win some. Lose some."

"Yeah."

"What else is wrong?"

"I didn't get to play—at all."

Bradford pats Niles on the knee. "That's probably because you can't play basketball with holes in your shoes."

Niles smiles. "I borrowed someone's shoes."

"Oh. Then how come you didn't play?"

"I'm not very good."

"You're a good baseball player," says Bradford.

"I'm okay. But I want to be a good basketball player."

"You made the team."

"I know. You're right. Thanks, Bradford."

"Niles?"

"Yes, Bradford?"

"You're not going to leave me in the woods like my old owner did, are you?"

"No, buddy. I won't ever leave you."

"Even when you're mad at me"

"Even when I'm mad at you."

"Can I have those peanut butter sandwiches now?"

With Niles's permission, Bradford *poofs* back to Niles's bedroom. And Niles makes a platter of sandwiches to share with his friend.

Chapter 8:

The next basketball game is today. Niles has been practicing his shots every night in the driveway. He goes to school. He goes to practice. He eats dinner. He shoots hoops. Bradford cheers from behind the garbage can. Niles doesn't mind as long as his Coach is not there to hear.

The Clearview Turtles are playing the Southside Tigers. Nick is sick, so Vinnie starts the game. It is close. The score bounces back and forth. At halftime they are tied.

"This is so awesome!" says Rashid.

"Do you think we will win?" Scotty asks Niles on the bench.

"I think we might."

"Do you think Coach Anderson will make us run if we lose?"

"Boys, be quiet, and watch the game," says Coach from his chair next to the bench.

Niles feels worse than he did the last game. Coach doesn't think he is taking the game seriously.

Bradford knows how Niles is feeling. He always knows when Niles is sad or worried. Niles made Bradford promise that he would not go to the game. Bradford always keeps his promises. However, it wasn't Bradford's fault that he had fallen asleep in Niles's basketball bag. It is a red bag after all. By the time Bradford woke up they were already at the gym. He thought about *poofing* to the family's car, but since he was already at the game, he thought he might as well stay. The bag is under Niles's feet. Niles sits in a chair next to coach. The bench is full of the other second-string players. Bradford needs a plan. He taps the top of his head. *Think. Think. Think.*

In the middle of the third quarter Coach Anderson starts to switch players. He takes out Luke and Abe and puts in Rashid and Sammy. After water breaks, Luke and Abe go back in. Vinnie makes a long pass to Cole. He goes around the defender on the other team and makes a lay-up. The Turtles are up by two points. Coach puts Scotty in for Tad. Tad slams his fist on the bench when he is taken out. He hates sitting on the bench.

"You're done, Tad." Coach Anderson is mad.

"What?"

"You heard me. Bad attitude=No more play time."

Tad hangs his head.

The cheerleaders get louder as the end of the game grows closer, especially the red-headed cheerleader.

"*Hey, Hey, Go, Go, Don't you stop. Don't be slow. You—can—do—it! Hey!*"

Bradford scratches his head. Scotty throws the ball out of bounds. Coach Anderson looks down the bench. He is choosing who to put in.

Just then Bradford leaps into action. He throws

out his little tail, activating the horns he rarely uses.

Moving as fast as he can so as not to be seen, he

takes out the legs of the bench. And all the way

down the line of players. The only player left

sitting upright is Niles, in a chair next to Coach

Anderson. Everyone else has fallen to the floor.

"I told you boys to pay attention to the

game!" He slams his clipboard on the ground while

the boys scramble to upright the bench, but it is no

use. The Clearview Turtles are up by two points.

The last-minute counts down on the clock. Coach

looks at Niles. "Niles, go in for Scotty."

Niles's eyes grow big. He is not sure if he is excited or scared out of his mind. "Yes, Coach." He runs to the check-in table. When the whistle blows, he runs into position.

Bradford watches from Niles's bag. His plan worked. Niles is in the game. Coach just needed a little *push* to see that Niles was ready and willing. Now, everyone will see if he is able.

Luke dribbles the basketball down the court. He passes to Vinnie. Vinnie shoots and misses. Cole makes the rebound and passes the ball out to Abe. The ball is knocked out of Abe's hands by the other team. They steal the ball. At the other end of the court, the team shoots the ball and misses. Niles makes the rebound. He shoots. He scores!

The crowd goes wild. But, something is wrong. The wrong side of the gym is cheering. Niles runs back to the other side of the court before he understands. He made a basket—for the other team.

Bradford hides his eyes behind his little hands.

Chapter 9:

The game is over. The Clearview Turtles won 48-47. Scotty went back in for Niles. He made the winning free throw. Luke and Cole put Scotty on their shoulders. He was grinning as big as Rashid.

Niles was excited for his team. But he felt terrible. He had never been so embarrassed in his whole life.

Before he left the locker room, Coach Anderson asked to talk to him.

"Yes, Coach?"

"Let me start by saying I am really proud of you for getting out onto that court tonight when I needed you. You always give 100% effort. You are a positive person. What happened tonight is not the first time it has happened."

"Really?" asks Niles.

"No way. If you promise to keep a secret, I will tell you a little story."

"I promise."

"When I was a sophomore in high school, *six years older* than what you are now, I did the very same thing—only worse."

"How was it worse?"

"I made a three-point shot."

"Oh," says Niles.

"Who won the game?"

"I honestly do not remember," says Coach. "But I never forgot that shot. My friends still give me a hard time when they see me every once in a while."

"That's awful," says Niles.

"I can laugh about it now," say Coach. "You will, too—someday."

"I don't know about that."

"Keep your chin up, Niles. It *was* a good shot."

Niles laughs about it a lot sooner than he expected.

His family takes him for ice cream again after the game. They toast their milkshakes to his first basket.

Chapter 10:

"How are you doing, buddy?" Bradford sits on the nightstand next to Niles's bed. He is clipping his toenails and throwing them on the floor.

"Bradford! Stop that! It's gross," says Niles.

. "Sorry, I did some damage today running on that gym floor at tip-top speed." Bradford smiles.

"Yeah, about that," says Niles.

"I know, I know," says Bradford. "But I didn't break my promise…"

"Yes, you did. You…"

Bradford puts up his hand to stop Niles. "No, I did not break my promise. I fell asleep in your basketball bag. It was not my fault. You should not have such a lovely smelling sports' bag. It's too tempting to use during nap time."

Niles sighs. "You still did not need to knock down the bench."

"I sure did. Yes…yes I did! Coach needed a reminder that you were ready to go into the game. And you made a basket, buddy!"

Niles looks at Bradford with squinty eyes. "Really, Bradford?"

"Hey, a basket is a basket." Bradford pushes the nail clippers to the floor. He jumps onto Niles's pillow. "You did good."

"Thanks, Bradford."

Niles turns off the light. Bradford *poofs* back to his red fuzzy sock bed. It has been a long day.

Niles dreams about shooting basketballs—
over and over. He makes some baskets. He misses
some baskets. It happens. Coach Anderson will put
him into more games. Niles is sure of it. And this
time he will be ready. Someday people will forget
his mistake. Or, someday, like Coach Anderson
said, he will laugh about it. Before falling into deep
sleep, Niles sinks a three pointer…in the right
basket. The crowd goes wild.

Please consider leaving a review on Amazon. Thank you.

Other Children's Books by Marcy Blesy:

Niles and Bradford, Baseball Bully

There are two things that nine-year-old Niles can count on when his family moves to a new town. One, his love for trying new sports will help him meet people. Two, his friendship with his pet dragon Bradford means he will never be alone. However, when a bully on the baseball team makes life hard for Niles, Bradford's idea of helping his friend gets him banned from the game.

Niles and Bradford, Basketball Shots

There are two things that nine-year-old Niles can count on when his family moves to a new town. A sport loving boy and his pet dragon. One, his love for trying new sports will help him meet people. Two, his friendship with his pet dragon Bradford means he will never be alone. However, when things do not go as well as planned during an important basketball game, Niles starts to doubt himself.

Niles and Bradford, Soccer Kicks

There are two things that nine-year-old Niles can count on when his family moves to a new town. One, his love for trying new sports will help him meet people. Two, his friendship with his pet dragon Bradford means he will never be alone. However, when a show-off soccer player steals the attention of Bradford, things go downhill for Niles.

Niles and Bradford, Track Team

There are two things that nine-year-old Niles can count on when his family moves to a new town. One, his love for trying new sports will help him meet people. Two, his friendship with his pet dragon Bradford means he will never be alone. However, an unexpected track injury and an unexpected new friend teach him the real meaning of a team.

Evie and the Volunteers Series

Join ten-year-old Evie and her friends as they volunteer all over town meeting lots of cool people and getting into just a little bit of trouble. There is no place left untouched by their presence, and what they get from the people they meet is greater than any amount of money.

Book 1   Animal Shelter

Book 2   Nursing Home

Book 3   After-School Program

Book 4   Food Pantry

Book 5:   Public Library

Book 6:   Hospital

Book 7   Military Care Packages

Dax and the Destroyers: (a new *Evie and the Volunteers* spin-off featuring a popular character)

Book 1: House Flip

Twelve-year-old Dax spends the summer with his Grandma. When a new family moves into the run-down house across the street, Dax finds a fast friend in their son Harrison. Not to be outdone by his friends, Evie and the Volunteers, and all of their good deeds, Dax finds himself immersed in the business of house flipping as well as Harrison's family drama. But don't expect things to go smoothly when Evie and her friends get word of this new volunteer project. Everyone has an opinion about flipping this house.

Book 2:   Park Restoration

Am I Like My Daddy?

Join seven-year-old Grace on her journey through coping with the loss of her father while learning about the different ways that people grieve the loss of a loved one. In the process of learning about who her father was through the eyes of others, she learns about who she is today because of her father's personality and love. *Am I Like My Daddy?* is a book designed to help children who are coping with the loss of a loved one. Children are encouraged to express through journaling what may be so difficult to express through everyday conversation. *Am I Like My Daddy?* teaches about loss through reflection.

Am I Like My Daddy? is an important book in the children's grief genre. Many books in this genre deal with the time immediately after a loved one dies. This book focuses on years after the death, when a maturing child is reprocessing his or her grief. New questions arise in the child's need to fill in those memory gaps.

Be the Vet:

Do you like dogs and cats?

Have you ever thought about being a veterinarian?

Place yourself as the narrator in seven unique stories about dogs and cats. When a medical emergency or illness impacts the pet, you will have the opportunity to diagnose the problem and suggest treatment. Following each story is the treatment plan offered by Dr. Ed Blesy, a 20 year practicing veterinarian. You will learn veterinary terms and diagnoses while being entertained with fun, interesting stories.

This is the first book in the BE THE VET series.

For ages 9-12

Be the Vet, Volume 2

What's it Like to Be the Vet